Samantha's WEDDING MEMORIES

A Scrapbook of Gard and Cornelia's Wedding

ILLUSTRATIONS   DAN ANDREASEN
STEP-BY-STEP ILLUSTRATIONS   SUSAN MCALILEY & GERI STRIGENZ-BOURGET

My Aunt Cornelia gave me this pretty scrapbook to hold my memories of her wedding forever and ever. It's a gift for being her "most exceptional bridesmaid"!

Ever since Aunt Cornelia and Uncle Gard became engaged, I've collected pictures and magazine clippings with all sorts of good ideas. We used lots of them to get ready for the wedding.

Still, you can't plan everything. Uncle Gard and Aunt Cornelia's wedding almost didn't happen…but I'm getting ahead of myself. Let me start at the beginning!

My dashing, daring Uncle Gard is always
off on a new adventure or trying out
the latest invention, like his newfangled
motorcar. He moves so fast, we thought
he'd never settle down!

My lovely Aunt Cornelia is more than
a match for Uncle Gard. With all her
ideas about changing the world for
the better, Uncle Gard has to step
lively to keep up with her!

When Uncle Gard and Aunt Cornelia were courting, they often came to Mount Bedford to visit Grandmary and me in Uncle Gard's rumbly motorcar. You could hear the **oowah, oowah** of the horn—and the engine's loud pops and bangs!—all the way down the street. The commotion upset Grandmary, but secretly I liked it. It was new and exciting and unpredictable—just like Uncle Gard and Aunt Cornelia!

I didn't like it so much the first time Cornelia spent Christmas with us. Grandmary wanted everything to be "fine and fancy" for Cornelia. I put up beautiful handmade snowflakes, but Elsa, our maid, took them down (and she wasn't very nice about it!). She said that my homemade decorations weren't good enough for Cornelia. Harrumph!

Cornelia's visit got much better when we went sledding. When Cornelia fell off the sled and landed in a very unladylike tangle, she just laughed and laughed. I could hardly believe it—a grown-up lady who knew how to play! I overheard Uncle Gard say to Cornelia, "I couldn't imagine life without you." That's when I knew they were in love!

Cornelia became my friend forever when she suggested
that we make a gingerbread house together. She had no
idea that Mrs. Hawkins didn't have time to help me make
one, or how disappointed I was by that. Cornelia just
seemed to know the things that make Christmas special.

Christmas Eve was perfect.
Everyone I loved most was
together, and we had the best time
singing Christmas carols while
Cornelia played the piano. Uncle
Gard sat next to her as they
played a duet, and their hands
kept touching. Grandmary didn't
seem to notice, but I surely did!

First, I want to say that I wasn't snooping. And I certainly didn't read anything! But after the carols, Cornelia asked me to bring her a book from her bedside table, and that's when I saw it: a heart-shaped silk pocket filled with love letters from Uncle Gard. Maybe she even has a lock of his hair!

Christmas was full of surprises, but this was the biggest one of all: Uncle Gard asked Cornelia to marry him and she said "Yes"! Now she wears a diamond ring on the third finger of her left hand. They say that the vein in that finger runs directly to the heart.

P.S. And...Cornelia asked me to be her bridesmaid!!!

I made Cornelia a sweet-smelling sachet for an engagement present. She can tuck it into her dresser drawer or hang it in her closet—maybe she'll even keep it with her wedding gown! It was easy to make.

Supplies
Pencil
Sheet of tracing paper
Scissors
Straight pins
5-inch-square piece of cotton fabric
5-inch-square piece of lace
Ruler
Thread to match fabric
Needle
Spoon
Potpourri
7-inch piece of ribbon, 1/8 inch wide

12

1. Use the pencil to trace the (heart sachet) on the facing page onto tracing paper. Then cut it out.

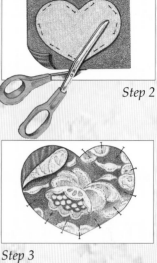

Step 2

2. Pin the heart pattern onto the *wrong side*, or back side, of the fabric square. Cut around the edge. Unpin the pattern. Pin the pattern to the lace, then cut out a heart from the lace in the same way.

3. Lay the fabric heart on the table with the *right side*, or front side, facing up. Then lay the lace heart on top. Pin the edges of the two hearts together.

Step 3

4. Backstitch the hearts together, ¼ inch from the edge.

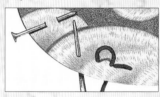

5. Keep stitching until there are 2 inches left open. Tie a knot close to your last stitch and cut off the extra thread.

Step 4

6. Unpin the fabric and turn it right-side out. Spoon potpourri into the sachet until it's plump.

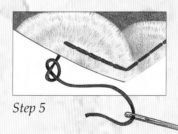

Step 5

7. Tuck the raw edges of fabric inside the sachet. Pin the edges together and finish sewing them up.

8. Remove the pins. For a finishing touch, tie a small ribbon bow and sew it to the top of the sachet.

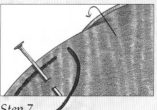

Step 7

Before the wedding, Cornelia hosted a luncheon for her closest friends, including Agnes, Agatha, and me—her bridesmaids! It's tradition to toast the bride and wish her all the happiness in the world.

The "bridesmaids' cake" was the most fun of all. Charms like these that told our futures were baked inside the cake. A horseshoe means good luck, a heart means true love, a baby shoe means lots of children, and a key means a happy home. I got the horseshoe in my piece of cake!

Agnes, Agatha, and I made tiny flower
baskets for everyone to take home from
the luncheon. We made sure to include
forget-me-nots, which mean "true love."

We made each of Cornelia's guests an elegant paper fan, too. Here's how we did it:

Supplies
Sheet of gift wrap, 30 by 4 inches
Ruler
Stapler
2 flat sticks, each 8 inches by ½ inch
White glue
Rubber band
12-inch piece of satin ribbon

1. Lay the sheet of gift wrap on a table with the back side facing up. Fold one end of the paper over 1 inch.

2. Turn over the paper and make another fold 1 inch from your first fold. Keep folding until you reach the end of your paper.

Step 2

3. Staple the fan together, about ¼ inch from one end.

Step 3

4. Glue 1 flat stick to one of the outside folds of the fan, ¼ inch above the staple.

5. Glue the other flat stick to the other outside fold in the same way.

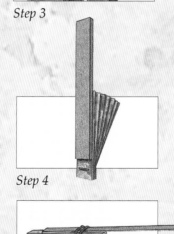

Step 4

6. Wrap a rubber band around the fan to keep it closed until the glue is dry.

7. When the glue is dry, open your fan. Tie the ribbon around the handle to keep the fan open, and untie the ribbon to close it.

Step 6

Cornelia wanted silhouettes of her bridesmaids for a keepsake of her wedding day. It was hard to stop giggling!

Supplies
Chair
Desk lamp
Table
Masking tape
2 sheets of white paper,
each 11 by 14 inches
Pencil
Scissors
Sheet of black paper, 11 by 14 inches
White crayon or piece of white chalk
Glue

1. Place the chair sideways about 1 foot from a blank wall. Place the lamp on a table about 5 feet from the chair. Shine the lamp onto the wall.

2. Seat your friend in the chair. You should see her shadow on the wall.

3. Tape a sheet of white paper to the wall so it catches your friend's shadow. You may need to move your friend or the lamp until the shadow fits onto the sheet of paper.

Step 3

4. When the shadow fits on the paper, use a pencil to trace the outline carefully. Make sure your friend sits very still!

5. After you've finished the outline, untape the paper from the wall. Cut out the outline. Then lay it on top of the sheet of black paper.

6. Use the white crayon or piece of white chalk to trace your friend's outline on the black paper.

Step 6

7. Carefully cut out the outline and glue it on a sheet of white paper. You've made a silhouette!

When Cornelia planned her wedding bouquet, she chose the flowers according to their meanings. There were so many to choose from!

Pansy
Thoughtfulness

Forget-me-not
True love

Blue periwinkle
Friendship

Primrose
Confidence

Rosemary
Remembrance

Magnolia
Love of nature

Honeysuckle
Generosity

Red rose
Love

Geranium
True friendship

Blue violet
Faithfulness

Daisy
Beauty

Orange blossoms

In her bouquet, Cornelia carried orange blossoms, a symbol that she and Uncle Gard will have lots of children. Orange blossoms are the most popular flowers for weddings!

Agnes, Agatha, and I carried lilac **tussie-mussies,** or small bouquets. Lilacs mean "first love." Cornelia chose them because Uncle Gard is her first love.

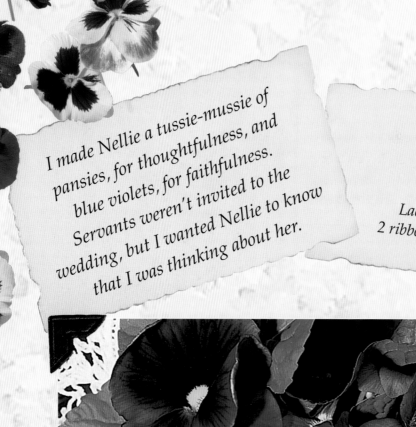

I made Nellie a tussie-mussie of pansies, for thoughtfulness, and blue violets, for faithfulness. Servants weren't invited to the wedding, but I wanted Nellie to know that I was thinking about her.

Supplies
Scissors
Flowers
String
Lace doily or hankie
2 ribbons, each 1 foot long

1. Cut off the leaves at the bottom of each flower, leaving 2 inches of bare stem.

2. Place the flowers and leaves in a pretty arrangement.

3. Tie the string in a double knot around the flower stems. Cut off the extra string.

4. Wrap the lace doily or hankie around the stems. Then tie it in place with the ribbons.

Steps 1 & 2

Step 3

Step 4

23

Agnes, Agatha, and I helped Elsa
fold fancy napkins for the reception.
It's easy once you know how!

*This one looks like a
bishop's hat!*

*Tuck in the sides to
make a blooming
flower.*

*Pull down the right and left
sides to make a butterfly.*

24

1. Lay a napkin flat on the table and fold it in half diagonally to form a triangle. Then turn the napkin so the folded edge is closest to you.

2. Fold the right and left corners up so they meet at the top point.

3. Fold the newly created bottom point up until it's about 1 inch below the top point.

4. Fold the same point back down to the bottom edge.

5. Carefully turn the napkin over, then fold the left corner about ⅔ of the way toward the right corner.

6. Fold the right corner over the left corner, and then tuck the point into the fold so the bottom forms a tube that will not pop open.

7. Stand the napkin up. With three points straight up, it is called a "bishop's hat," named after the tall hats worn by Catholic bishops.

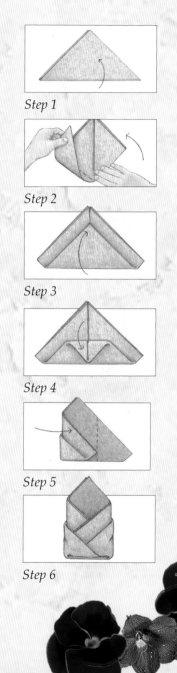

Step 1

Step 2

Step 3

Step 4

Step 5

Step 6

Uncle Gard and Aunt Cornelia's wedding cake was cut and packed in pretty little boxes tied with ribbon. Guests took boxes of the wedding cake as souvenirs. If this were my cake, I couldn't bear to cut it!

Cornelia spent weeks being fitted for her wedding gown and deciding on accessories. She followed the saying, "Something old, something new, something borrowed, something blue, and a silver sixpence in her shoe."

Cornelia's pearls were a gift from Uncle Gard. They were her "something new"!

Cornelia helped me make a hairbow that matches my bridesmaid dress exactly!

Supplies
Scissors
1¼ yards of stiff ribbon,
2 to 3 inches wide
French clip barrette,
at least 1½ inches long

Step 1

Step 2

Step 3

1. Cut the ribbon into 3 equal pieces.

2. Take 2 of the strips. Fold the ends of each strip into the middle to form two "bows."

3. Lay 1 of the bows across the other at an angle, scrunching them in the middle.

4. Open the barrette. Center the bows over the top part of the barrette.

5. Tie the third strip around the bows and the top of the barrette. Cut each end of the ribbon into a V shape.

6. Fluff out the bows, and your hairbow is ready to wear.

Step 4

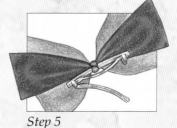

Step 5

Step 6

When I tried on my beautiful bridesmaid dress for the first time, I let out a shriek of delight! Cornelia's mother, Mrs. Pitt, worried that I wouldn't behave properly as a bridesmaid, but I would never embarrass Cornelia—and especially not on her wedding day.

Cornelia's dress was even fancier than this one! It was decorated with lace and tiny pearls, from its high collar to its deep hem.

Cornelia's veil was made
of lace as light and as fine
as mist. It was absolutely
perfect. Cornelia said, "I'll
wear it only once, to mark
the happiest day of my life."

We found some old lace curtains and used them to make pretend bridal skirts and veils. Cornelia's littlest sister, Alice, wanted to play bride, too. We were out of curtains, so we gave Alice a pillowcase instead. I promised her that the next time we played dress-up, she'd have a better skirt and veil. That seemed to satisfy her. But then…

Cornelia's face turned as pale as a ghost when she saw Alice coming downstairs draped in the wedding veil. Alice had hacked it in two and used one part for a skirt and the other part for a veil. Cornelia's veil was completely, utterly, and totally ruined. Mrs. Pitt said that we'd have to postpone the wedding!

There was no time to get a new veil, but I had an idea. I raced to find my mother's veil and got back just in time to save the wedding. I'll never forget how beautiful Cornelia looked as she walked slowly down the aisle—or the special wink that she gave me!

With my memories tucked safely in this scrapbook, I'll never forget anything about Aunt Cornelia and Uncle Gard's "most exceptional" wedding.

Visit our Web site at **americangirl.com**.

Printed in China.
04 05 06 07 08 09 10 11 12 C&C 12 11 10 9 8 7 6 5 4 3 2 1

The American Girls Collection®, Nellie™, Nellie O'Malley™, Samantha™,
Samantha Parkington®, and American Girl® are trademarks of American Girl, LLC.

PICTURE CREDITS
The following individuals and organizations have generously given
permission to reprint images in this book:

pp. 10–11—engagement ring, courtesy of Paula Moon-Bailey;
pp. 14–15—bride's lunch, *Bridesmaids' Dinner,* 1905, Museum of the City of New York,
Byron Collection; pp. 26–27—wedding cake, printed with permission from
Colette's Wedding Cakes, © 1995, Little, Brown and Company; bridal garments,
Wisconsin Historical Society; pp. 30–31, wedding dress, ice-blue linen
with cream floral foliate damask sub-pattern, ca. 1908–1918,
Museum of the City of New York, gift of the Visconti/Nizza family.

Illustrations by Dan Andreasen
Step-by-step illustrations by Susan McAliley and Geri Strigenz-Bourget

Cataloging-in-Publication Data available from the Library of Congress.